This book belongs to:

WITHDRAWN FROM STOCK

Published by Ladybird Books Ltd
A Penguin Company

Penguin Books Ltd, 80 Strand, London WC2R 0RL, England

Penguin Books Australia Ltd, 250 Camberwell Road, Camberwell, Victoria 3124,
Australia

Penguin Books (NZ) Ltd, Cnr Rosedale and Airborne Roads, Albany, Auckland, New
Zealand

This book is based on the TV episode "I'll Fly Away", written by Steven Sullivan,
from the animated TV series *Miss Spider's Sunny Patch Friends* on Nick Jr, a
Nelvana Limited/Absolute Pictures Limited co-production in association with
Callaway Arts & Entertainment, based on the Miss Spider books by David Kirk.

First published by Ladybird Books 2005

1 3 5 7 9 10 8 6 4 2

LADYBIRD and the device of a ladybird are trademarks of Ladybird Books Ltd.

Printed in China

I'll Fly Away

David Kirk

Everybuggy in Sunny Patch was so excited. The Flying Aces were in town! Dragon couldn't wait to see Rocky and Roxie, the leaders of the troop.

High in the sky, the Aces flew
forwards and backwards. They
did figure eights and loop-de-
loops.

"Buggin'!" gasped Dragon.
"I wish I could do that!"

Rocky landed on a nearby
tree stump.

"Howdy kids! Who wants to get
a taste of the sky?"

All the little bugs raised their
arms. The Aces invited Bounce
to come for
a ride.

"Be careful with Bounce!"
Dragon exclaimed. "We've been
through everything together.
We're best bug buddies for life!"

"You should join our school," Rocky said. "With a little practice, you could be a Flying Ace in no time!"

"Really? *Me*?" cried Dragon.

That night Dragon told his mum
he wanted to join the Flying Aces.

"I don't think so, Dragon," said
Miss Spider. "You're a part of our
family now. You can fly away some
other day."

Dragon sighed and
slumped off
to bed.

Dragon couldn't sleep.

"Are you leaving us?" asked a
tearful Bounce. "I thought we
were best bug buddies for life."

"We are," said Dragon, "but I'm
a dragonfly. I should be with
other dragonflies!"

The next day, Miss Spider and
Holley discussed what Dragon
had said.

"Maybe he's right," sighed Miss
Spider. "Maybe he does belong
with other dragonflies."

Though they didn't
want to let
Dragon go,
they
decided
to let him follow
his dreams.

The Sunny Patch kids gathered around the Hollow Tree to say goodbye to Dragon.

Bounce was the saddest of all. "Don't forget your best bug buddy!" he called.

Miss Spider and Holley gave
Dragon a final squeeze.
"We love you, Dragon," they
said.

Dragon squeezed them back.
"I love you too," he said. Then,
looking at the clouds, he took
off to meet Rocky and Roxie.

Dragon practised his moves with the Aces. He learned to fly in formation, to make beautiful figure eights, and a perfect loop-de-loop. But he didn't feel happy. He couldn't stop thinking about his family.

At the Dribbly Dell, Squirt, Shimmer, and Bounce were trying to start a soccerberry game. But without their star player Dragon, it wasn't much fun.

Suddenly, they heard the sound
of wings.

"Dragon's back!" yelled Bounce.

"But Dragon," began Holley, "you wanted to be with other dragonflies!"

"I thought I did," replied Dragon. "They may be dragonflies, but you're my family."

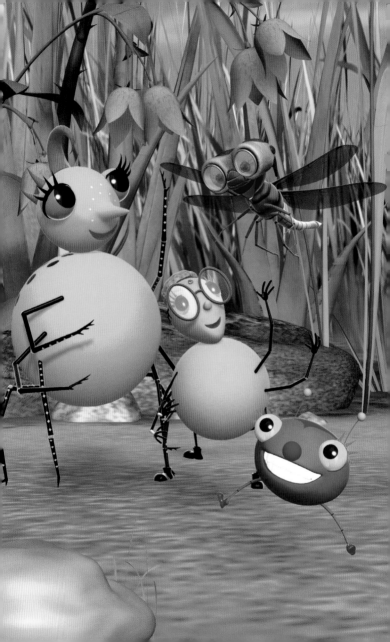

Everyone cheered.
The happy family
was together again.